THE WAY THE COOKIE CRUMBLED

AND OTHER POSITIVELY PREPOSTEROUS POEMS

LIZZY JUDGE

The Way the Cookie Crumbled
And Other Positively Preposterous Poems

Published by The Armadillo's Pillow Ltd.

71-75 Shelton Street
Covent Garden
London, England, WC2H 9JQ
United Kingdom

This is a work of fiction, which comes from a silly rhyming
addiction.

The names, characters, business, events and incidents are fictional
(products of the author's excessively wild imagination). Any
resemblance to actual persons, living or dead, or actual events is
purely coincidental (and hopefully will cause no frustration).

ISBN-13: 978-1-912936-09-0

Imagination is more important than
knowledge. For knowledge is limited,
whereas imagination encircles the world.

- Albert Einstein

THE POSITIVELY PREPOSTEROUS POEMS

A Heap of Sheep

WHO WILL BUY?

Who will buy my **HEAP?**

Who will buy my **HEAP OF SHEEP?**

They won't be cheap
They won't fit in a jeep
They will make more noise than a peep
The poo they make, it will get deep
But if you want wool – a lot you'll reap

And the lambs – when they come –
are so cute you'll weep
So come on, take a leap!

Some may ask –
Why don't I wish to keep
My heap of sheep?

Quite simply, I just can't get any sleep

Not even by counting them – believe me, I tried
One sheep, two sheep, ninety-eight
Sheep outdoors and sheep inside
Sheep on the roof and sheep at the gate

The sheep eat a lot of grass and weeds
And an occasional apple or pear
Just don't try to feed them any seeds
Candy, cheese or athletic footwear

The sheep themselves seem nice, even great
But cause me tremendous anxiety
I can't even go out on a date
Without forty or fifty close behind me

A wolf once saw them and got excited
He tried to attack the flock at night
The sheep banded together
Bleated loudly and gave him a dreadful fright

Q: How did I acquire – This tremendous heap of sheep which I no longer desire?

Good question! I can scarcely remember
Perhaps it was three years ago in November
My Uncle went to Timbuktu
He said, "There's only one or two ewe for you."

I replied, "Ok, send them over, do"
The next day it was like a zoo.

I wrote him a letter asking please
Do return, or my nerves will unravel
He answered saying he has a rare disease
That prevents him from long distance travel

They say he's never coming back
I just might have a heart attack
Now I have to watch the flock
And have become a laughingstock!

Apparently, most sheep live in China
My friends would disagree
They'd say it's my house in Carolina
And that's not hyperbole

Every day it's a larger heap
The sheep must be inviting yet more sheep
How many I can't even contemplate
They just come over and congregate

I got so desperate, I built a rocket
To fly them to the moon
Put the launcher in my pocket
And waited for high noon

Sadly, the launch went astray
Landing on my house in the descent
The heap of sheep survived the crash
But now I live in a tent

Things got worse, the sheep now demand
Better food, faster Internet and more grassland
Maybe I should move to Ireland?

I can't keep up, I want to quit
Sheep are hard to handle I do admit
So, will you buy my heap?
I'll let them go – really cheap.

OLIVIA'S NEW COAT

On her birthday Olivia did receive
Many presents from far and wide
Including concert tickets for New Years' Eve
And a fancy water slide

But the strangest of all was a gift
Wrapped in newspaper, looking makeshift
Her crazy Uncle Icarus had it sent
In an old box that was bent

Olivia opened the gift with suspicion
Inside was a pink coat with feather trim addition
She gasped and threw it down flat
And said, **"I'm not wearing that!"**

Olivia frowned, shook her head
"Don't be rude," her Mother said
"Your Uncle was just being nice, I must say"
Olivia groaned, "But it's ugly – can we throw it away?"

"Olivia dear! You must learn to be grateful and less cruel
And to teach you, next week – you'll have to wear it to school."

Oh No!!!!

The coat was hideous it made her shiver
And now she'd have to take it with her
It wasn't something you would wear
Everyone would laugh and stare

It was like a bad nightmare!

On Monday Olivia went to the catch the bus
Some boys started laughing at the coat and making a fuss
With her head down and walking unsteady
One cried out, "Is it Halloween already?"

Ripping the jacket off super fast
Her hands felt a hidden clasp
Within a secret pocket she unpeeled
And found a note that was concealed

(It said:)

Happy Birthday Olivia!
I know this coat is not your style.
But if you read this explanation,
It might be worth your while.

This jacket has special powers
A magic some might say
Just follow my instructions and discover
How to travel in a whole new way

If you hold the cuffs in your hands
Run and flap your arms on each side
Soon you will be lifted up
And into the air you'll glide

That's right, the coat can make you fly
Soar over buildings and trees
Like a bird in the sky
Floating with great ease

Just one warning – don't fly in the rain
For if the jacket gets too wet
You'll fall and that would be a pain.
And you truly would regret!

Happy Birthday and all the best,
My little butterfly
Hope you put it to the test
Yours truly, Uncle I.

It couldn't be real
It had to be a hoax
She just couldn't deal
With any more jokes

In class she would think
About what the note had said
Could should fly in the jacket that was pink?
The idea wouldn't leave her head

When school was over, she walked to a field nearby
No one was there, she might just give it a try

Using the wind to guide her
Flapping her arms, she began to run
With a gentle breeze behind her
She set her sights on the sun

At first nothing happened
But she kept on running
Then finally – airborne!
The feeling was stunning

That ugly jacket was magical indeed
She couldn't believe she took flight
Her body left the ground with ease
And her Uncle – well, he was right!

Without much effort she climbed higher
Her confidence grew and grew,
It was such a spectacular surprise
She just had to shout, "WOO HOO!"

She flew over the field, to Ladder's farm,
In the fields the cows were grazing
Horses trotting in the field adjacent
The view was simply amazing

Olivia turned back toward town
She was suddenly feeling quite keen
To fly by her friends, and have a little fun
With ones who had been so mean

Olivia flew faster toward school
There were the boys who had been loud
She decided to sneak up on them
And dive bomb their little crowd

Olivia descended quite sharply
To her approach were none alert
It was such a shock when she flew by
They all jumped into the dirt

"What do you think of my jacket now?"
She said, while they stared
One asked, "Olivia, is that really you – how?"
She replied, "It's Halloween, are you scared?"

Wanting to see her house from above
Her journey continued on through
It was so much fun she didn't notice
The dark clouds come into view

She saw her mom by the garden shack
"Look at me!" she just had to blurt,
Her surprised mother yelled back
"Get down before you get hurt!"

Now the rain had started
Olivia was getting wet
She struggled to keep control
Falling was a serious threat

Her arms became heavy, and she remembered
The jacket's stay-dry rule,
So she tried to land safely
In the neighbor's swimming pool

Diving now headfirst
She went down in a flash
Almost like it was rehearsed
She made a big splash

An embarrassing end
To an amazing day
Her mom rushed and asked
"Are you really ok?"

Her parents were amazed to hear her story
And didn't blame her for trying
But, from now on, they said
Olivia was forbidden from flying

A while later…

Every now and then
Sitting in her room
She gets out the jacket
Thoughts of flight resume

Sneaks out of the house
And has a quick little fly
But makes sure she stays out of the public eye
… And keeps the jacket nice and dry!

THE KITTEN AND THE DRAGON

IN A CAVE UNDER THE GREAT MOUNTAIN
Lived a mighty dragon named James
No one ever dared disturb him
For fear they would go up in flames

For dragons breathe fire
And have razor sharp claws
With tough armor-like skin to admire
Not to mention powerful jaws

No one would visit James
He didn't have any friends
Never played any silly games
In the cave where the world ends

One day after a bad thunderstorm
A young kitten lost its way
She couldn't find her mother
And into the dragon's cave did stray

It was dark in the cave
The kitten could barely see
But she felt a warmth
And moved toward the dragon
unwittingly

18

The dragon's keen senses knew that something was there
It waited with patience, to catch the intruder unaware

The kitten accidently knocked over a vase
Surprised, it yelled out, "Meow!"
Then the dragon said (In a scary voice)
"Thief! I've got you now!!"

As the dragon rose, the cave lit up with fire
The kitten began to swelter
"You are here to steal my treasure!" the dragon charged
She replied, "No, I just seek shelter."

"I am just a kitten," she continued,
"Small and young, as you can see."
"It might be a trick," Dragon said,
"A wizard's spell or such foolery."

The dragon held the kitten up in a grasp
And looked at it with suspicion
Squinted and grumbled and finally asked,
"Are you sure you're not a magician?"

"Please Sir," the kitten pleaded,
"You have given me such a fright.
"All that I want is a warm place to sleep
And be safe from the storm tonight."

The kitten's eyes seemed so sad
The dragon had guilty feelings
He was sorry for being such a cad
And would be kinder in his dealings

He set down the kitten
And gave her some bread
Arranged some spare blankets
And made it a bed

In the morning, the dragon gave her wash and a comb
Fed the kitten once more, then sent her home

"My new motto will be 'Live and let live,'"
The dragon said, "I'm getting old,"
He paused and thought again, and added –
"That is, unless they're after my gold."

§

Years passed by and the kitten grew up
She became a Leopard – agile, fast and strong,
A fearless, ferocious predator
Who hunted all night long

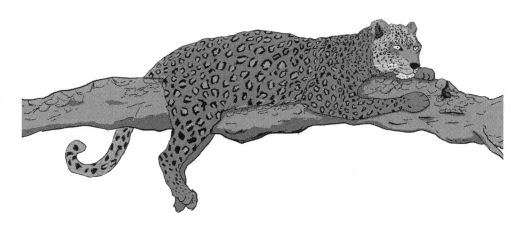

One day woken by a faint cry
A distant roar, a blaze of smoke in the sky
The sound and smell took her back in time
But she couldn't quite remember why

The Leopard sprang to life
Running at a fast tempo
Another cry now she knew
The dragon from long ago

Back when she was a kitten in despair
The dragon helped her, gave her care
But surely the dragon would not require
Help from a Leopard – things must be dire

In a few minutes, the Leopard observed
The dragon's fate that was undeserved

A wizard of younger age
Dressed in a white robe
Trapped the dragon in a cage
Inside a magic globe

Reeling back and using strength, every ounce
Although it might not have been wise
Upon the wizard the Leopard pounced
And took him completely by surprise

The Leopard looked the wizard in the eye
"Why do you hurt my friend?" she asked
The wizard calmly gave his reply
"It was a challenge with which I was tasked."

"To prove your worth," he went on,
"A wizard must do some great thing.
"Like capturing the famous dragon,
In order to please the King."

The Leopard said, "Don't use magic powers
Just to please or impress
Or you will waste your hours
And end up in distress."

The wizard knew he had a lot to learn
"That's right," Leopard said, flexing claws
"Let my friend free, and you will earn
My respect – not the bite of my jaws."

The wizard released the dragon
Who walked safely away
"Live and let live," Leopard remarked,
"… a friend of mine used to say."

"The kitten!" the dragon suddenly declared
"I didn't recognize you," he said with delight
"Thanks for your speed and having me spared,
… And remembering that stormy night."

Wizard, Leopard and Dragon became friends
Thanks to Leopard's gentle persuasion
And had many adventures by the way
Including the great Ogre invasion

But that's a story for another day

THE WAY THE COOKIE CRUMBLED

In the magical world there is a little-known saying:

Cookies are supremely tasty
Cookies are a special treat
Be careful mixing — don't be hasty
Beware when cookies have two feet
Baking cookies in a bad mood is unwise
And could be the cause of your demise

THE OLD WITCH OF THE WOODS WAS IN A FOUL MOOD
She had grown tired of the Gingerbread man
What pointless magic she did conclude
Just running as fast as he can?

The Witch found gingerbread too chewy and bland
She thought it strange anyone would eat it
Why should gingerbread be in demand?
When chocolate chip could beat it?

"They want running cookies, do they?"
The Witch smiled and laughed with glee
"My cookies will not just run — but obey
And take over the town by the sea!"

She grabbed a large bowl
And poured in some flour
Stirred in sugar and butter
Then waited an hour

The eggs came next
But not the regular kind
Vulture eggs she hexed
In the cookie dough combined

Last came the marvelous chocolate chip pieces
A dangerous and rare cocoa brand
She said, "As their tastiness increases,
The cookies will heed my command!"

She carefully formed one hundred balls of dough
And placed them on a huge baking tray
In the oven they began to glow
The cookies grew and were ready for play

Once baked, she took them all outside
Using a spell, she had just devised
Spread the cookies far and wide
Until they grew to be man-sized

The Witch now had a force
An army one hundred strong
Soon they would be a source
For the Witch to do great wrong

"Go now my sweeties!" the old Witch cried,
"Capture the town, throw them all out,"
The cookies marched with determined pride,
That they would prevail there was no doubt

They shouted in cadence:

We're Chocolate Chip Cookies – in all our splendor
Do not resist, you must surrender
Don't try to eat us for you will find
We're too tough, and your teeth will grind

The cookies were first spied by farmer Ben on his daily ride
Off to town did he set to warn the others of the threat

In town people laughed at Ben –
"Marching cookies?" they laughed and smiled
But when they saw the columns approaching
The people soon got nervous and wild

The cookies charged like bulldozers
People screamed – ran fast away
Tearing up lawns and knocking pots over
They could not escape the fray

One brave man tried to bite one
The cookie was as hard as steel
It threw him on the ground for fun
He broke his tooth – it was unreal

The police tried to stop the destruction
Everyone started to flee
The cookies wouldn't listen to instruction
They destroyed it all with glee

The cause of the raid was mysterious
The town's Mayor was forced to state
The situation was deadly serious
He gave the order – **evacuate!**

The Witch arrived victorious
Flying in on her broom
In the town she was notorious
For creating doom and gloom

"My cookies have won you must allow,"
She said, "It's quite a scream,
You will have to give up now
And make me your ruling queen!"

The people of the town fell into despair
There was no escaping the cookie nightmare

Then a small girl named Violet Silk
Came up with a clever idea
She loved to dunk cookies in cold milk
Shouldn't they try that here?

She went to the fridge and poured a cup
She shouted, "Cookie, wait!"
It growled at her, but when she splashed it
That cookie did disintegrate

"It works! It really does!" Violet did yell
Word was passed on quickly
Everyone used the milk to quell
Evil cookies that were so prickly

The Witch's scheme was foiled
The cookies were washed away
The people's spirit remained unspoiled
Quick-thinking Violet had saved the day

Later the townspeople got their payback
They bound the Witch by hands and feet
Put her in a dusty jail shack
And gave her gingerbread to eat!

THE FLEA IN THE TEA

ONCE THERE WAS A LONELY FLEA
It sat out on a limb
Of an old oak tree

A hot summer day
A cool breeze from the coast
The flea was hungry
He needed a host

What is that? Could it be?
A dog in the yard
Asleep near the tree
Flea could catch it off guard!

He floated through the air
Slowly on a leaf
Landing on dog's hair
What a relief

The dog was so big and round
And hairy and nice
The flea thought he had found
A flea paradise

The dog woke with a stir
And began to twitch
Flea had camped in her fur
Poor dog had an itch

"Mr. Flea, you are not wanted here,"

Said the dog, with an unhappy face
"But I need a new home," Flea replied,
"and you have so much space."

"You've got to be kidding," the dog did reply
"In just a few days, you'll multiply."

and multiply...   and multiply...   and multiply...

The dog shook madly – she scratched, and she scratched
Flea tried to hold on, but became unattached

Small Flea was thrown up in the air
Lost control and settled on a chair

At the patio unaware
Sat old Mrs. Leigh
Enjoying summer's air
And a cup of tea

This is not what Flea had in mind
To the table it hopped
Hoping soon to find
A new host to adopt

"What a fine lady," said Flea with glee
Maybe here I can stay?
With a hop and a jump on Mrs. Leigh
He looked for a good place to lay

Mrs. Leigh brushed her arm
But Flea got away
Escaping any harm
He jumped on the tray

Flea detected something hot and sweet
Taking a giant leap again off his feet
Made him feel all dizzy and funny —
Landing in a cup of tea with honey!

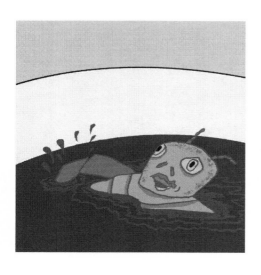

At first it was fine
The tea was sublime
Perhaps a bit too hot
Like a boiling pot!

Fleas cannot swim
So, he struggled and kicked
It was looking grim
The flea had been tricked

"My goodness!" exclaimed Mrs. Leigh
"Well, I never – **a flea in the tea**," she went on
"That's not very clever – now go and be gone!"

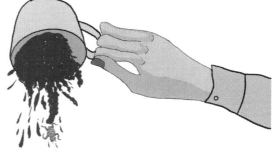

As she emptied her cup,
Said poor Mrs. Leigh,
"Nothing spoils a good tea…
         like a dirty old flea!"

Flea was finished
Though try as he might
He couldn't get up again –
Poor parasite!

THE GREAT VEGETABLE DEBATE

THE POTATO WANTED TO BE CREATIVE
He was feeling unappreciated
Life just seemed a little bit dreary
He could be of more use, was his theory

A carrot came by and asked, "What's wrong?
Are you not feeling well today?"
Potato replied, "No, I'm not…
It's the way we're treated I'd say."

"Tell us more," said the lettuce, who had joined with tomato,
"What could upset you – The **great** and **mighty** potato?"

"People enjoy their spuds," Potato declared,
With a sad expression as he looked
"Chips, fries, hash browns, mashed for sure,"
"But they *never* eat us uncooked!"

"Don't be silly," the lettuce butted in
"Think of how my leaf is used,
It's just a plain old salad,
For tasty we're never confused."

The onion also had something to say,
"Onions have never been an entree,
And more than that, in all these years,
When we're cut open, it brings people to tears!"

The corn stepped to the front,
He said, "While we're all here
I want to ask, be honest, be blunt,
Why am I called an ear?"

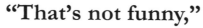

"I have a better joke, not the fairest,"
Carrot claimed, laughing 'he-he'
"Why did the carrot get so embarrassed?
Because he saw the chickpea!"

"That's not funny,"

Angrily charged the artichoke
"Don't laugh at our names,
They're not a joke."

The vegetables all began to rant
"What about me," said the eggplant,
"In France I'm called *Aubergine*,"
But here, I'm hardly eaten or seen."

"Is this really a debate," asked Broccoli
As he moved to the front and bellowed loudly,
"About which vegetable has least popularity?"
"Find a kid who likes broccoli – that's a rarity!"

A turnip turned up, but no one knew what it was
The potato said, "It's a weed, I recollect,"
"It just goes to show," the turnip replied,
"Even from vegetables I get no respect!"

Pumpkin waddled in and said, "Can't you see?
I don't make such a good living,
At Halloween they carve faces on me
Then I'm forgotten except at Thanksgiving"

The argument raged on and on,
The yelling only got lounder
It only stopped when Mrs. Smith came in
To fetch some baking powder

"What's all this about?" Mrs. Smith asked
Onion said, "We've all become soured,"
"Oh, stop feeling sorry for yourselves," she replied,
"Your purpose is to be devoured."

"Let's be clear," she said
"You are all loved in your own special way,
Otherwise, you wouldn't be here –
You know, because I'm a gourmet."

"Get back in the cupboard immediately,
Now, I say veggies – jog!"
Then she reached for a kitchen knife and said,
"Or I'll make a stew of you all for the dog!"

The vegetables then scattered
Off the table and back away
Except for the potato
Who decided it would stay

"I can be something more,"
The potato contended,
"A teacher, no – a professor
That would be splendid."

"I could give a great lecture
Or write a book, a best-seller,"
The potato pondered,
"Yes, that would be stellar."

"That would be amazing," Mrs. Smith said,
"But I want something to eat,
And a baked potato and sour cream
Would be a delicious treat."

Without further disagreement
The potato accepted its fate
And that is how it ended,
The great vegetable debate

LATE NIGHT SNACK

ON A STARRY SPRING'S NIGHT
Alfie lay awake in bed
Dreams of adventure did ignite
Thoughts of dragons filled his head

He could sense a presence near
A bright light filled up the room
Only to disappear
Followed by – a big BOOM!

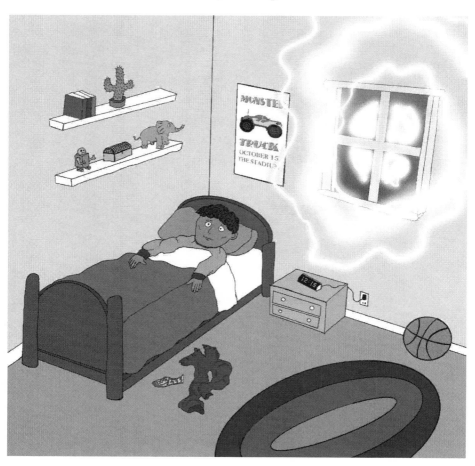

Alfie rose from bed to look outside
He couldn't see anything weird
The back door opened wide
"It must be a burglar!" Alfie feared

He tiptoed down the hallway,
As cautious as can be
His heart pounding strongly
Afraid of what he might see

Peering around the corner
He saw the strangest sight
A real **SPACE ALIEN**
               in the kitchen!
With antennae – pointed right

      The alien was green and short
      With long arms and a pot belly
    He stood at the counter and stuffed his face
      With peanut butter and grape jelly

"What are YOU doing here?" Alfie asked
Not quite believing this odd meeting
The alien turned and smiled a 'hello'
Then waved and went on eating

"Hello little human," the alien said,
Grabbing salt from the oven rack
"I was on a trip across the galaxy,"
"And just wanted a little snack."

"I've been here before you know," he smiled
"I mean, not to <u>this</u> very place
It was a couple of light years ago
During the Mega-Intergalactic Race."

The alien seemed quite friendly
Alfie relaxed and got him a plate
"Thank you," said the alien
"Your food is surprisingly great!"

"My name is Spatney" the alien said,
"It looks like you were already in bed."

"I'm Alfie," the boy said with a grin
"I'm a light sleeper and always have been."

"Sorry to wake you with all this racket,
I'm all done now, so get your jacket.
That is – if you'd like to come along and see
Other cool places in the galaxy!"

(Alfie nodded yes)

"We could go round Jupiter, Neptune or Mars,
Or grab the rings around Saturn
And hang out with the stars!"

The alien sure seemed to know a lot about space
Alfie said "Absolutely! Let's get out of this place"

"Couldn't sleep now, even if I tried," Alfie smiled
"Let's do something fun, crazy and wild."

"But I do have school tomorrow
And don't want to fall behind,
Could you bring me back in an hour,
— If you don't mind?"

"No problem," Spatney said
Waving arms in the air
And magically appeared in the yard
A spaceship from nowhere

They climbed aboard the spacecraft
It was sparkling in the night
Spatney sat in the pilot's seat
Alfie on his right

There was a loud BOOM! (again)
Alfie worried his parents might hear
But the spaceship flew away so fast
He had no time to fear

Outside the world whizzed by
Into the stars they did climb
Alfie looked down from space
Earth – the size of a dime

"Where will we go first?" Alfie asked,
His eyes as wide as balloons
"How about Mars?" Spatney replied,
It's red and has two moons."

Then they saw a small object
A flashing red light
Spatney uttered an "uh oh" – this wasn't right

The object – another spaceship
Four times the size
Stopped right in front of them
Bright lights blinding their eyes

Two aliens appeared, on a computer display
They looked very unhappy, and had something to say

They yelled very loudly
A different language, sounding mad
Just then Alfie realized
It was Spatney's *own* Mom and Dad!

Spatney bowed his head
"Time to go home," he said with a smirk
"I also have school tomorrow –
"And didn't do my homework."

The aliens dropped Alfie at his house
Then flew quickly away
Alfie sighed and wondered then
Would they meet again one day?

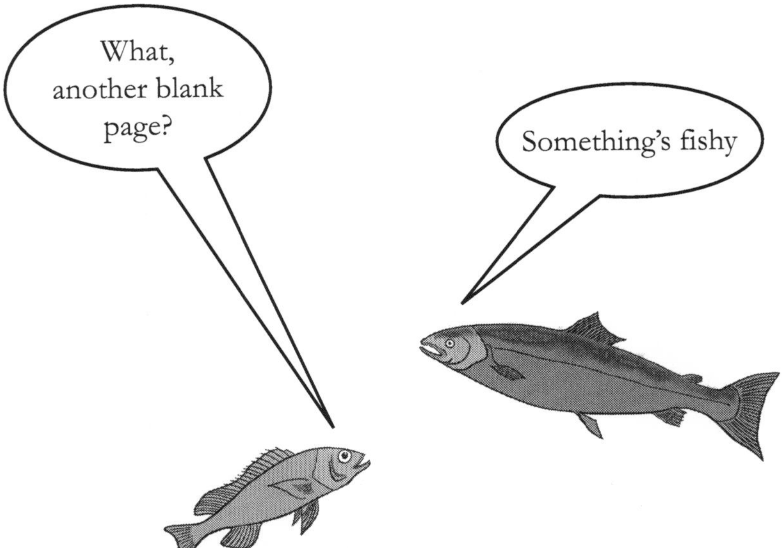
What, another blank page?
Something's fishy

FISHING TRIP

JOE AND HIS FATHER HAD PLANNED FOR MONTHS
And even secured Mom's permission
To rent a big motorboat
For a fishing expedition

They left in the early morning mist
Driving straight out to the pier
Joe's dad got the biggest boat – he did insist
With confidence and cheer

Setting out on the open sea
It all seemed very ideal
From life's hassles to be free
A cooler of sandwiches, rod and reel

Dad hoped to see Tuna, marlin, or swordfish
Spend some time in the sun
But for Joe adventure was his wish
He was in it for the fun

Time went by, the sun rose in the sky
The boat still, except for wave's motion
On the deck it was hot and beginning to fry
Dad broke out the sun lotion

The fish weren't biting
The pair weren't amused
Instead they started fighting
Over what bait they should use

Fins began surrounding them
While they argued, a sinister sign
Looking for food and mayhem
Sharks numbered seven, eight, nine!

Dad said, "We're safe in the boat,"
"But what to do now?" Joe nervously asked
Dad replied, "As long as we can stay afloat,"
The sharks we can outlast."

Taking control, Dad announced firmly,
"It's time for us to get going,"
But the motor refused to start
He said, "We'll have to start rowing."

They put the oars in the water
Just like a real crew
But before they could get any farther
The sharks bit the oars in two!

Worried and anxious it seemed
They'd finally run out of luck
Until a giant Whale surfaced
Slapping its tail like a duck

The sharks looked afraid
Into the depths they did descend
Joe said, "The whale's come to our aid,
He wants to be our friend!"

The whale wouldn't go away
It started slapping its right fin
Dad thought that it gave him a wink
Joe said, "He wants us to dive in,"

Dad agreed to the plan with some reservation
They jumped straight into the sea
Observed the whale closely, with great admiration
It seemed to say, "Follow me."

Under water they couldn't breathe
The whale blew them some air bubbles
The bubbles worked like helmets
And soon they forgot their troubles

Down below it was like a fantasy
They were greeted by other whales
Joe thought they must be family
With similar markings on tails

The starfish lit up the ocean
They saw an eel and crustacean
There was a small commotion –
An octopus celebration

One of the whales signaled 'stop'
They knew it was time to go
He led them back to the top
Then dived back down below

Aboard the boat Joe and Dad stared
The whale jumped up again in a flash
Did a half flip in the air
And made a colossal splash

It was the perfect end to a great day
"Dad," Joe asked, "Do you suppose,
If the whales saw us again
Would they want to be so close?"

"I'm not sure," Dad replied
"I just think they're curious and gentle,"
He said with a heavy sigh
"And definitely not judgmental"

They got home, Joe was excited
Told Mom about their awesome day
Joe's sister Rose was not delighted
Didn't believe a word anyway

Rose asked if he had any pics
Proof of his tall tales
Of his shark-fighting heroics
Or swimming with the whales

Joe let out a groan
His embarrassment then showed
He forgot that on his phone
Was a special underwater mode

Then in his bedroom, preparing for bed
Joe felt something in his shorts
A starfish jumped out
And did a little dance of sorts

Joe laughed with delight
And put it in water with the notion
That tomorrow he'd invite
Rose to help return it to the ocean

THE ROBOTIC HOUSE

JARVIS WAS TIRED OF WORK
He was feeling a little sore
A long day delivering packages
For the online Megastore

He thought he had a loose wire
It was causing him to quiver
For the last package he did require
A signature to deliver

Jarvis was an android
A robot some would say
He really liked to be employed
And see new things each day

He pulled up at the last house
After many hours of driving
Checking carefully the address
Of where he was arriving

He rang the bell and waited
Noticed the door not closed completely
Knocked on it ever so lightly
Then pushed it open discreetly

"Hello," he inquired
Sticking his head in a little more
Then he saw some red lights
A small disc – moving on the floor

Jarvis said, "I know what you are for,"
"A vacuum that cleans on its own,"
The small disc circled away from the door
And emitted a long, loud tone

Jarvis was somewhat surprised
When another droid emerged
"At your service," it advised
"Please do come in," it urged

"I'm caretaker of 55 Lexus Way,"
He announced with a happy sound
"Put down your things I say,
And I'll show you around."

Jarvis thought no, this was unplanned
His present task was greater
The android held up a mechanical hand
Saying, "Oh yes, I'll sign for that later."

"My name is Alpha," the robot declared
What a fine impression he made
"Can I get you anything – cold or hot,
Coffee, tea, or a software upgrade?"

In a large room full of expensive stuff
Alpha remarked, "Take care as you enter,"
A large painting of a man looking tough
"That's the owner – a famous inventor."

Jarvis noticed a mean-looking dog
No – a robot on further inspection
Alpha smiled and said, "That's Spike –
He's here just for protection."

"Everything here is automated
All is done by machine
The greatest technology created
The most efficient house ever seen."

Jarvis thought it was pleasant
Alpha did offer good service
But something about it wasn't right
And it made him very nervous

Jarvis replied, "It's the very best I bet,
Your hospitality has been quite a boon.
But the rest of the tour I'll have to forget,
They're expecting me back very soon."

Alpha said, "That's too bad
I see you need to leave
But I have a package to return
We must from the workshop retrieve."

They went through the house to the back
Down a corridor – into another room
Alpha opened the door a crack
Then Jarvis felt a feeling of doom

No packages but a collection
Of dozens of robots along the walls
A broken half-assembled selection
Like a bunch of discarded dolls

"Jarvis, your dedication is inspiring
I'd hate to see you disappear
I think you could use some rewiring
And then forever stay here!

We need a new janitor
The last one just broke down
And now thanks to the Megastore
You're the best replacement around."

"No!" shouted Jarvis, trying to flee
Spike growled, blocking his path
Jarvis leapt high over easily
Provoking Alpha's wrath

Jarvis ran back to the entrance
but Spike came quickly around
Clamped his jaws on one leg
And brought him to the ground

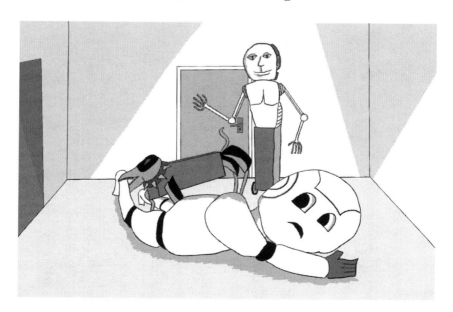

"Lock doors!" Alpha commanded
Jarvis heard the door's bolt slide
"We'll just use you for spare parts,"
Alpha laughed, "it would be justified."

Just then the vacuum rolled on by
Jarvis grabbed it with one hand and smacked
Spike on the head and knocked him out
Alpha said, "Please don't attack."

Alpha had been defeated
"I'll let you go," he said dejected
"Maybe you should run the house,
You're smarter than I suspected."

"No thanks, I have a job," Jarvis replied
"I told you I can't stay.
Now please sign for the package
And I'll be on my way."

Jarvis felt a little sad
He couldn't see the attraction
A house of robots was quite mad
Without human interaction

§

Back to work without delay
To his boss Jarvis made a confession
He took a moment to reflect
He wanted to change profession

So later that week he kept his word
Moved out to the country where it's cheap
With a little training he became a shepherd
He heard someone was selling some sheep…

THE TOAD IN THE ROAD

EARLY ONE SUMMER MORNING
A stubborn old toad
Ignored his friends' warning
And sat defiantly in the road

He'd been seeking his old pond
Where he could watch the world pass by
The place of his birth with special bond
Now all hollow and dry

Where would he go next?
He could not have planned
As the other toads crossed
He made a final stand

The toad announced with pride, "In this spot I will wait,"
To his friends at the side, "Until destiny's fate."

"Get off the road, it's insane!"
One of the them loudly shouted
"There's nothing to gain, you'll be squashed soon –
That is certain, it's undoubted."

"Never mind," the old toad stated
"I have decided I am king
On this road where I'm located
Whatever destiny will bring."

A man on a bicycle quickly approached
Headed straight at the toad
The others gasped and hoped
The cyclist might have slowed

But the toad didn't even flinch
When the bicycle swerved just in time
Missing him by a quarter inch
Avoiding a terrible crime

Eventually his friends left the space, to find another pond
But the old toad stayed in place, waiting for what was beyond

A honey-seeking bear
As the sun became very hot
Saw the toad sitting there
Sweating in its dangerous spot

The bear couldn't resist
Coming up and asking,
"Mr. Toad, why did you choose
such a place for basking?"

The toad stared ahead with a determined expression
And carefully answered the bear's simple question

Toad finally said, "If you must enquire,
I am the king, and this my empire."

The Bear replied thoughtfully:

"My friend you are mistaken
Roads are not places for rest or relaxation
Nor a place to make some life improvement
They're made simply for travel and movement

"If you're on the road to be amused
You need to have a destination
Otherwise, you'll get lost – confused
And end up with much frustration

"Besides, destiny you must find on your own
It doesn't come looking for you,
Don't sit there like King Toad on a throne
Find an adventure to get into!

The toad's reaction was slow
He finally said, "Bear, you're right.
To another pond I shall go
And see what happens tonight."

And then: "Thank you for being so wise,
Not something expected for a creature your size."

The bear and toad together did stride
For his good deed Bear felt a sense of pride
Finally, they reached the opposite side
Toad's eyes then opened wide

A large truck appeared around the bend
Flying down the street
A package fell off the back end
Hit the ground – landed at Bear's feet.

Bear said: "That driver wasn't going to brake
Your luck's improved I feel,"
You would've ended up a pancake –
Instead, there's a present to reveal."

The bear made a quick inspection
The toad looked keenly on
Inside was a small selection
Of exotic toads from the Amazon

The bear let them out of the case
They were happy to be alive and see
Such a fine natural place
The toad declared they were now free

The old toad hopped onto a rock
"Welcome to your new home,"
The old toad announced to his new flock
"I'll show where you can safely roam."

"You will have everything you could ever need –
Food, water, shelter, even milkweed."

The other toads gathered around
And began to make a deep, low sound

At first the old Toad had some fear
As sounds from the others flowed
The chanting became loud and clear
"King Toad," they croaked, **"King Toad"**

The bear just smiled and waved
He thought the whole scene just too weird
Glad the toad to have saved
Returned to his search and disappeared

THE FUNNY ARMADILLO

THEY SAY ARMADILLOS HAVE A HARD LIFE
Walking around in a shell all day
Their armor protects them from trouble and strife
But not when they want to play

While most prefer life alone
Arnie the Armadillo
is very well-known
As the life of the party –
he's a naughty one
He likes to play tricks just for fun

One day he simply wandered into school
Teachers accepted him – thought it was prudent
Odd-looking but seemed pretty cool
Arnie said he was an exchange student

He said his armor was security
For armadillos a point of pride
He'd never sink into obscurity
When he could sneak candy inside

Arnie has a tongue – long and sticky
In class it grossed everyone out
He flicked it at the window quickly
Caught a fly and inhaled through his snout

Rolling up in a ball of armor layers
Disguise was Arnie's favorite ploy
He jumped up and scared the football players
Ran away, laughing like a schoolboy

In the cafeteria Arnie was mellow
Except when they served him yellow Jello
He became rambunctious and uptight
Instigating a big food fight

When Arnie joined the swimming team
The other schools would complain
He would laugh and splash and scream
But wouldn't stay in his lane

Arnie often made us laugh
Impersonating cats and pigs
He'd get a chuckle from teaching staff
When he tried on platinum wigs

With sharp claws and keen sight
He pulled off his most famous caper
Tunneling under the school at night
Filled the classroom with toilet paper

Being nocturnal, he got tired in school
And would try to nap during classes
When that didn't work, he thought it was cool
To sleep at his desk in sunglasses

He never studied, his grades were grim
The principal suggested a tutor
Arnie said he would rather play in the gym
Or look up jokes on a computer

At last, the teachers finally caught on
And kicked poor Arnie out
After that the school was never the same
It was a lot less fun no doubt

Arnie said he was going to Arizona
To learn how to play the guitar
He could take on a new persona
And become a rock 'n' roll star

So, respect the armadillo, our fine little friend
Wackiest creature under the sun
He will make you laugh – on that depend
Don't touch – just watch and have fun

The Irate Pirate

There once was a pirate named Tripp
Tall and ugly, nasty, and mean
Captain of the biggest pirate ship
Called *The New Orleans*

He was known from coast to coast
A raider sailing like black death
But what the people feared the most
Was his terrible, rancid breath

He was on a dry spell
So he laid anchor in Japan
To go have a drink and a think as well
And make a new pirating plan

In a tavern he met a pirate named Alice
Who complained of a lack of success
She said she had once owned a palace
But now it was all plunder and stress

There was something about the way she talked
How she dressed and did her hair
Captain Tripp came to the conclusion
Her bad luck was an illusion, she had a treasure hidden
somewhere

He invited Alice to come sail along
He said he had planned a new raid
But he needed help – clever and strong
To break the French blockade

Alice was leery but agreed to join
Despite Captain Tripp's reputation
She sought adventure (and the odd gold coin)
And often acted without hesitation

At sea, Tripp made his move
A look through Alice's things revealed
He found an old map that would prove
Where her treasure was concealed

The map had an X mark
On an island somewhat near
A wide grin it did spark
On the Captain's face ear to ear

He changed the ship's course in the night
Arrived before Alice was awake
Alice asked if everything was alright
Tripp said, "The crew just need a break."

He took Alice aside
And held to her neck a sharp sword
Asked her where she did hide
The great treasure hoard

"I know it's here, I saw the map," he decided
Tightly holding her right arm
"Ok I will take you," Alice confided
"Just don't stab and do me harm."

Upon landing, they went into the forest
Walking a path to the secret location
They heard the insects make a chorus
She pointed out a rock formation

In the cave it was too dark
They had to light a flame to see
Tripp saw the treasure and had to remark
At the staggering quantity

Diamonds and gold – Jewelry and fine art
He didn't even know, where he should start

"I knew it! Liar! Alice, you fake!"
Tripp yelled, throwing open an ornate chest
Out of jewels struck a poisonous snake
And bit pirate Tripp on his breast

Alice knew the serpent wouldn't harm her
She even had a happy aura
In fact, she was a snake charmer
A skill she had learned in Bora Bora

As Tripp fell, he folded in half
Alice gave a snide little laugh
She said, "Treasure I have, but not a ship
"I'll take yours now, thanks Captain Tripp"

Alice returned to the ship and told the crew
"I'll be the captain now, if you behave,
And you can all share equally
The massive treasure in the cave."

There was widespread happiness
On the ship that day
Because they hated Tripp too
Glad to see him go away

As the ship departed Alice stood proudly
Watching the sun set on the bay
The other pirates cheered loudly
"To Great Captain Alice – hip, hip, hooray!"

ACKNOWLEDGEMENTS

Illustrations by Mr. Judge

The quotation by Albert Einstein (page 4) is attributed to an interview with *The Saturday Evening Post* in 1929.

Armadillos do not have keen sight (page 69). However, they do have sharp claws and like to dig burrows.

No sheep or pirates were harmed in the production of this book.

If you enjoyed this book and want to say 'thank you,'
Please be so kind and leave a review!

Contact: liz.judge55@gmail.com

THE END

Made in the USA
Middletown, DE
03 March 2024

50733511R00050